READ-IT-YOURSELF stories are ideal for children learning to read on their own.

Introducing Sophie Rabbit, the lovable leading character in these warm, humorous stories about first encounters of school and friendship.

In *Sophie and Abigail*, it's Sophie Rabbit's first day at school and she's both excited and anxious. She soon makes a great new friend, Abigail, but what happens when Abigail moves away?

**Kaye Umansky** was born in Plymouth and worked as a primary teacher for a dozen years. Now a full-time writer, she lives in London with her husband, daughter and two cats.

**Anna Currey**, who grew up in Ireland, has drawn and painted for as long as she can remember, particularly animals and plants. She lives in Wiltshire with her husband and two teenage daughters.

For Ella – KU

For all my nephews and nieces – AC


**The Sophie Rabbit books:**

Sophie and Abigail

Sophie and the Wonderful Picture

Sophie and the Mother's Day Card

Sophie in Charge

First published in Great Britain
in Gollancz Children's Paperbacks 1995
by Victor Gollancz
A Division of the Cassell group
Wellington House, 125 Strand, London WC2R 0BB

Text copyright © Kaye Umansky 1993
Illustrations copyright © Anna Currey 1993

Edited by Belinda Hollyer    Designed by Herman Lelie
Produced by Mathew Price Ltd
The Old Glove Factory, Bristol Road, Sherborne
Dorset DT9 4HP, England

The right of Kaye Umansky and Anna Currey to be identified as
authors of this work has been asserted by them in accordance with
the Copyright, Designs and Patents Act, 1988.

A catalogue record for this book is available from the British Library.

ISBN 0 575 06017 4

Printed in Singapore

# Sophie

## and Abigail

### Kaye Umansky
### Illustrated by Anna Currey

GOLLANCZ CHILDREN'S PAPERBACKS

LONDON

The day that Sophie Rabbit started school for the very first time, she was too excited to eat her breakfast.

"Eat up, Soph," said her dad.

"Leave her, George," said her mum. "Her tummy knows best. Feed the baby, Louise, there's a dear, while I find Sam's football shorts."

Sophie's brother and sister went
to big school now. They were always
talking about their teachers and
friends. Sophie listened to their
stories with tall ears. She simply
couldn't wait to start school herself.

But when Sophie finally arrived
at Briary Infants she suddenly
felt very shy, and clung tightly
to Mrs Rabbit's paw.

"Will you stay?" she whispered.

"A little while," said her mum,
with a comforting squeeze.

But Sophie knew that her mother
couldn't stay long, because she had
to get back to baby Gareth.

Mrs Badger, the teacher, showed Sophie her coat peg. Then Sophie's mum gave her a hug, and had to go. Sophie had never felt more alone in her life. And then . . .

"Excuse me," said a small voice. "Can you see a dormouse peg anywhere?"

Sophie looked down. A tiny dormouse was staring up at her.

"This one's yours," said Sophie, pointing it out.

"Could you put my hat on it? I can't reach. By the way, I'm Abigail."

"Of course," said Sophie, holding out her paw. "I'm Sophie. I'd like to help."

And so the great friendship began.

"I've got a friend," announced Sophie that night. "She's called Abigail."

"Who?" asked her dad.

"Abigail. She's a dormouse."

"Big name for a dormouse," said George Rabbit.

"That's nice, dear," said Mrs Rabbit,
spooning mashed turnip into Gareth.

"So?" said Sam. "I've got hundreds of
friends."

"Me too," said Louise. "Thousands."

"I don't care," said Sophie happily.
"I don't want more friends.
Only Abigail."

And that was the way of it. From that
first day on, Sophie and Abigail
did everything together.

They played in the sandpit
and on the see saw.

They held paws on nature walks.

They saved each other chairs
at circle time.

They shared apples and biscuits
and secrets. Sometimes, other animals
would try to play with them, but both
Sophie and Abigail thought it was more
fun on their own.

"Can Abigail come to tea?"
asked Sophie a few weeks later.

"Who?" asked her dad.

"Abigail," explained Mrs Rabbit.
"Sophie's friend. Yes dear, she can
come – tomorrow, if you like. I'll buy
some buns. George, see to Gareth,
would you? He's choking on a
cabbage leaf."

But the following morning, Abigail
wasn't in school.

Sophie kept looking at the door
to see if Abigail would arrive late.
But she didn't.

The other animals were busy playing,
and didn't seem to notice that Sophie
was on her own.

That night, there were too many buns
for tea.

The next morning, Mrs Badger took Sophie to one side.

"Bad news, Sophie," she said. "Abigail's family has moved to the other side of the wood to look after her sick grandad. Abigail won't be coming to this school any more."

"Never?"

"I'm afraid not. But don't be too upset, dear. There are lots of other nice little animals to play with."

But it wasn't the same without Abigail. At circle time, nobody saved Sophie a chair. And at playtime, there was no one to sit on the other end of the see saw.

"What's up, Soph?" asked Sophie's dad that evening. "You look a bit down in the whiskers. Can I help?"

So Sophie told him about Abigail, and how much she missed her.

"And no-one wants to play with me. They've all got their own friends."

"Poor old Soph," said George Rabbit. "It's always hard to lose a friend. But Mrs Badger's right. Making new friends can be hard sometimes, but it's worth it in the end."

"Are you sure?" asked Sophie.

"I am."

"But supposing Abigail forgets me?"

"She won't."

The following morning, Sophie missed
Abigail terribly. But at circle time
Gordon Fox offered her his chair,
and Kelly and Fran, the Mouse twins,
asked her to play dressing up, so
the time went quite quickly.

And then something unusual happened.

A new frog arrived, called Graham.

He wasn't sure where to put his scarf.

"There's a free peg next to mine,"
Sophie told him.

"But it's got a dormouse on it," said
Graham.

"It belonged to my friend Abigail,"
said Sophie. "And I'm sure
she wouldn't mind."

When Sophie got home that day, there
was a surprise waiting for her.

"There's a letter for you," said
George Rabbit. "It came by the
afternoon post. I think it's from that
friend of yours. Er . . ."

"Abigail!" Sophie reminded him,
tearing it open excitedly.

And this is what it said.

Hazel View
Mossy Bank
Other side of Wood

Dear Sophie

Please come to
tea on Sunday.
I will show you
my new room
Grandad is getting
better.
Do you like buns?
love from Abigail xxx

P.S. I miss you

"I've had a letter from Abigail,"
Sophie announced happily to Graham
Frog the next morning. "I'm going to
tea with her on Sunday."

"Really? That's nice," said Graham.
"Fancy a go on the see-saw?"

And together, they ran out into
the sunshine.

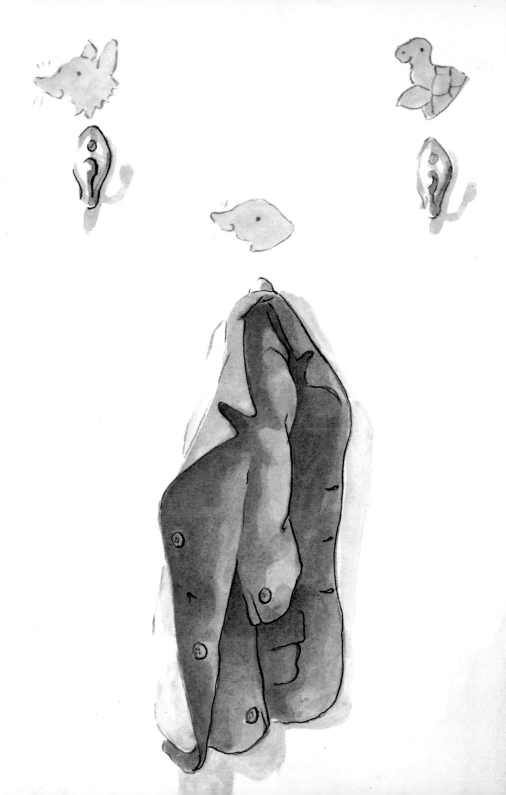